ALIENS

THE DOG'S DINNER

Collect all the books in the *GUNK Aliens* series!

JONNY MOON
GUNK
ALIENS
THE DOG'S DINNER

First published in paperback in Great Britain by HarperCollins *Children's Books* 2009
HarperCollins Children's Books is a division of HarperCollinsPublishers Ltd
77-85 Fulham Palace Road, Hammersmith, London W6 8JB

The HarperCollins website address is:

www.harpercollins.co.uk

1

Copyright © HarperCollins 2009
Illustrations by Vincent Vigla
Illustrations © HarperCollins 2009

ISBN: 978-0-00-731096-8

Printed and bound in England by Clays Ltd, St Ives plc

Special thanks to Colin Brake,
GUNGE agent extraordinaire.

A long time ago, in a galaxy far, far away, a bunch of slimy aliens discovered the secret to clean, renewable energy...

... snot!

(Well, OK, clean-*ish*.)

There was just one problem. The best snot came from only one kind of creature.

Humans.

And humans were very rare. Within a few years, the aliens had used up all the best snot in their solar system.

That was when the Galactic Union of Nasty Killer Aliens (GUNK) was born. Its mission: to find human life and drain its snot. Rockets were sent to the four corners of the universe, each carrying representatives from the major alien races. Three of those rockets were never heard from again. But one of them landed on a planet quite simply *full* of humans.

This one.

CHAPTER ONE

Jack Brady was hungry.

Actually he was more than hungry – he was very hungry. Very, very hungry indeed. Hungry enough that he might even have said he was starving, only his mum had once shown him some people in Africa on the news who *really* didn't have anything to eat, and had explained to him exactly what starving meant. So now he tried not to use the word 'starving' if he could help it.

But he *was* very hungry.

Jack was on his way home from school. Not for the first time, he hadn't managed to eat any of his school dinner. He didn't dare tell his mum. He knew she paid good money for him to have a hot meal at lunchtime – she told him often enough – but the food was just too disgusting. And Jack knew a lot about disgusting things. He was, after all, an agent of GUNGE, the ultra-secret organisation that protected the whole planet from the threat of hordes of horrendous aliens.

Jack – and his friends Oscar and Ruby – had already had two close encounters with extraterrestrials working for GUNK – the Galactic Union of Nasty Killer Aliens. With the help of Snivel (a robot dog who doubled as an alien trap and had an extra eye due to a design mistake) and Bob, their unseen contact at GUNGE, they had outwitted and defeated the Squillibloat and the Burrapong and now Jack was awaiting his next mission briefing. What he really wanted right now, however, was a burger and fries. Or a slice of pizza. Or anything at all that he could eat!

"Hey, Jack!" said a familiar voice suddenly, dragging Jack's thoughts away from food. It was Bob! Jack looked around him, but there was no sign of the GUNGE agent. Previously Bob had spoken to Jack from a rubbish bin and a postbox but the street that Jack was walking along had neither. Jack didn't know how Bob did it, but somehow the GUNGE controller had the ability to hide his base inside tiny spaces. Jack assumed it was some kind of alien technology that GUNGE had managed to get their hands on. The question was: where was Bob today?

Jack looked around again. He was on the parade of shops between school and home. There was a small supermarket, a newsagent, a florist's shop and a bank. Where could Bob be?

"Over here," said Bob more urgently. "The cash point."

Jack hurried over to the hole-in-the-wall cash point at the front of the bank. Luckily there weren't many people about.

"Is that you, Bob?" he whispered.

"Of course it is," said the voice of Bob from within the cash point machine.

Jack stepped closer to the machine and put his hands over the keypad as if he was about to tap in his secret code, just like he'd seen Mum do loads of times.

"I guess you want us to go after alien number three," said Jack.

"Absolutely," replied Bob in a serious tone, "and there's not a moment to be lost. We must get the rest of the Blower."

The Blower was a sort of intergalactic phone that the aliens needed – if they got hold of it, it would allow them to summon their armies to come and steal all the human race's snot.

For the aliens of the GUNK alliance, snot was the key to everything – the energy source

they needed to power all of their technology. There were four alien races in the Galactic Union of Nasty Killer Aliens, a union forged with one purpose only: to seek out new sources of that most precious resource – snot. GUNK had dispatched scout ships to every corner of the known universe. Every ship carried a representative from each of the four races. And each individual alien carried one part of the Blower. The four alien races really didn't trust each other so this was the only way to secure the union.

Not long ago, one of the alien scout ships had discovered Earth, where they found the human race to be a natural source of the snot they craved.

Luckily, the ship had malfunctioned and crashed, separating the four aliens and, of course, their four

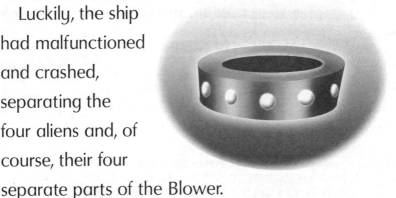

separate parts of the Blower.

Jack and his friends had captured two of the aliens and delivered them and their parts of the Blower to Bob already.

"But you've got half the Blower now," Jack reminded Bob, "surely the other two can't work on their own?"

"It's not as simple as that," Bob explained. "If the Blower parts aren't linked on a regular basis each can issue a distress signal. That signal isn't as powerful as the one that the whole Blower can send but it would be strong enough to reach the GUNK home planets.

The only way to keep the existence of Planet Earth a secret is to capture all four parts of the Blower."

"All right," said Jack. "So who are we after now?"

"The creature with the third part of the Blower is called a Flartibug," said Bob.

Jack couldn't help but giggle at the name.

"It's not funny," insisted Bob, sternly.

"Of course not," replied Jack, giggling again.

"Snivel's been uploaded with everything you need to know about the creature and its disgusting habits. I hope you have a strong stomach, Jack, you'll need it for this one."

As if in response to Bob's words Jack's tummy rumbled loudly.

"As a matter of fact right now I've got an empty stomach," Jack confessed. "I don't suppose you could make this machine give me some money, could you? If you did I could get myself something to eat on the way home."

"Nice try," said Bob, "but no can do. If I start giving away money I might blow my cover. Off you go."

With his stomach still rumbling with hunger Jack headed for home. He'd need to summon the others.

As well as being a GUNGE agent, Jack was also an inventor. He loved nothing more than fiddling around with bits and pieces to make prototypes of his latest ideas. Recently he had been working on remote-control flying machines. After spending some time on a remote-control Frisbee he was currently developing a new and improved helicopter.

When he got home Jack made himself a quick toasted-cheese sandwich to deal with

his hunger and then ran up the stairs to his room. He pulled out his latest experiment from its storage place under his bed. It was a magnificent model helicopter, built from bits and pieces scavenged from a dozen different kits. Jack's hybrid helicopter was designed to fly higher and carry a greater weight than any of the ones you could buy off the shelf in the model shop.

Jack opened his bedroom window and placed the chopper on the windowsill. He then fixed the payload carrier – an old hamster exercise ball – to its landing gear. He ripped a piece of paper from the back of his school rough book and wrote a quick note to his friend Oscar – *Meet me in the tree house ASAP* – and then stuffed the note inside the ball. Now he was ready.

Jack picked up the remote control and started up the little helicopter's engine. It lifted into the air and flew perfectly, under Jack's careful piloting, towards the house

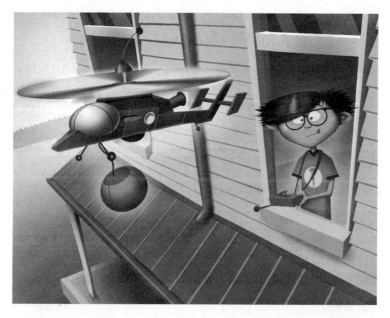

that backed on to Jack's back garden. This was where Oscar lived. Jack carefully negotiated his flying machine through the branches of the tree at the bottom of Oscar's garden and around the shed suspended in the tree, which was their base of operations. Finally the chopper approached Oscar's bedroom window.

Jack bit his lip. Now for precision flying – one mistake and his precious experiment would be smashed to pieces.

Carefully Jack made the helicopter bump gently into the window. Back and forth, back and forth; the chopper tapped quietly on the glass. Would it be loud enough for Oscar to hear? Suddenly the window opened and Jack wrestled with the controls to back the aircraft out of the way of the glass. Oscar appeared at the window and saw the helicopter hovering there, with the ball hanging underneath it.

Pressing the joystick, Jack flew the helicopter forwards so that Oscar could reach out and take the message. He read it and then gave a big thumbs-up sign to Jack. Mission accomplished.

A few minutes later the pair of them were
in the tree house. Oscar held up the helicopter.

"Your latest invention?" he asked.

"Yep," said Jack.

"What's so special about it?"

"It can lift really heavy
weights," said Jack.

Oscar pulled a face. "Wow.

That'll come in *really* useful," he said sarcastically.

Jack ignored him, pulling another gadget out of his pocket. "Now to get Ruby over here," he announced.

Oscar was peered at the small black object in Jack's hand. "What's that then?" he asked. "Modified GPS? A radio transmitter?"

Jack waved it under Oscar's nose.

"Mobile phone," he said and, laughing, began to dial Ruby's number.

CHAPTER TWO

It didn't take long for Ruby to reach them. Less than ten minutes after making the phone call Jack and Oscar heard a loud crashing sound from somewhere below the tree house.

"That sounds like Ruby," said Oscar with a grin.

Ruby was a girl, but she wasn't like most of the girls at Oscar and Jack's school. She

both the boys' interests: she
d gadgets as much as Jack did
and she loved any kind of dangerous
sport, the way Oscar did. If anything,
she was even more of an adrenaline
addict than him – she was forever
trying her hand at all sorts of wild
activities, but always while keeping
it secret from her mum.

Jack and Oscar ran to the door of
the tree house and looked down.
Below them there was a large hole
in the hedge that ran between Oscar's
garden and the alley.

The hole was Ruby-shaped.

Ruby herself, dressed in knee- and elbow-
pads and a helmet, was standing on a
skateboard in the garden. Jack saw that Ruby
was holding on to a string and was pulling in
a large kite attached to the other end.

"I've been trying kite-boarding,"
she yelled up at them, while wrapping
the string deftly round a handle.

"Does your mum know?" wondered Oscar.

"Course not," replied Ruby, grinning. "She
thinks I'm pony-trekking!" She sniffed, then
took a tissue from her pocket
and wiped her nose. "Actually,
my mum wanted me to stay in

today, because I'm getting a cold. But I convinced her that my pony needed brushing."

Jack saw that beneath her knee pads she was wearing jodhpurs.

Having finished wrapping up the string Ruby placed the kite and skateboard at the bottom of the tree and began to remove a large heavy belt.

"What's with the utility belt?" asked Jack, noticing that the belt was decorated with wide pockets that looked full of heavy objects.

"Ballast," said Ruby, but with her blocked nose the word came out strangely.

"No need to be rude, he only asked!" replied Oscar.

"Ballast," said Ruby more slowly, dropping the belt on the ground. "This is an adult-size kite, if I didn't weight myself down like this, I'd be flying!"

"Sounds cool!" said Oscar, wide-eyed.

"Yeah, *flying* would be cool, but how would you land safely, doughnut?!"

Ruby started climbing the ladder to join the lads in the tree house.

"So what's up?" she asked. "Another alien?"

"Let Snivel explain," said Jack.

A few minutes later the three of them were settling down inside the tree house, ready for Snivel's briefing.

Snivel was a poor abandoned dog that Jack had adopted.

At least, that's what Jack's mum thought.

In reality Snivel was a sophisticated robot made using alien technology acquired by GUNGE operatives. Most of the time he looked like a relatively normal dog (albeit a rather scruffy one with three eyes) but at the right command from Jack he would transform into an alien trap.

Oh, and he ran on snot, instead of batteries.

The third eye was a design flaw that Jack was beginning to find endearing. Snivel, on the other hand, said it made his vision blurry and gave him a headache.

Snivel sat in front of the three kids and pressed a concealed button behind his ear. Instantly a holographic image was projected from his nose into the air in front of him. Jack and the others had a brief glimpse of a revolting-looking insectoid creature before the hologram flickered, and disappeared.

Startled, Jack turned to Snivel. The robot dog's eyes were half-closed (all three of them) and he was swaying on his feet.

"Need… power…" said Snivel. "Need… snot."

Jack gasped – Snivel hadn't had any food since he'd eaten one of Jack's sneezes two days before! Jack turned to Ruby. "Your snotty tissue," he said. "Hand it over."

"You're kidding," said Ruby.

Jack just looked at her.

"You're *not* kidding," she said, sighing. Then she took the tissue from her pocket and handed it to Snivel. The Snotbot began licking the snot from it.

"Oh, gross," said Oscar.

Snivel looked up, his eyes wide open now. "Got any more?" he asked Ruby.

"I'm getting a pretty bad cold," said Ruby. "There'll be plenty more where that came from."

"Fantastic," said Snivel. "Your snot is prime stuff."

Jack and Oscar stared at him with disgust.

"Can we please get on with it?" Oscar asked.

Snivel nodded. There was a whirring sound, and then the projection started up again.

The alien displayed in the blue light of the hologram was the most disgusting thing the

kids had seen so far in their GUNGE careers. It looked a bit like a giant cockroach with a multitude of long thin hairy legs and thin insect wings protruding from its back. Its head was covered in smeared food, like a baby eating chocolate.

But even on the holographic image, the gang could see that it wasn't chocolate the alien was eating. It was a mess of decaying mulch. A thick soup of rotting vegetable matter dripped from the disgusting creature's mandibles.

"It's called a Flartibug," explained Snivel.

Oscar laughed out loud.

"It's called what?" he asked.

"A Flartibug," said Snivel again.

This time Ruby and Jack joined in the laughter. Oscar repeated the name, making the most of the sounds.

"Flartibug!" he giggled.

"There's nothing funny about the Flartibug, I assure you," insisted Snivel in a huffy tone.

"Except his name," muttered Oscar, laughing so hard that tears began to roll down his face.

Snivel tried not to notice the laughter of the children and continued his briefing.

"The Flartibug," he continued, "lives on a planet that is totally covered with rotting, mouldy vegetation."

"Bet that stinks," said Jack.

"It's universally known as the smelliest planet in civilised space," said Snivel.

"So it likes stinky places?" asked Ruby.

"And it eats the most revolting food imaginable," continued Snivel.

Oscar managed to stop laughing for a moment.

"I know exactly where we'll find him then," he said, grinning,

"we need to check out Greasy Joe's!"

Then, slightly ruining the dramatic moment, Ruby sneezed.

"Ooh," said Snivel. "Save that for me."

Greasy Joe's was a café on the edge of town not far from the main road. Officially it was called Joe's Fast Diner but everyone in town knew it as Greasy Joe's and avoided it like the plague. Joe's customers were exclusively lorry-drivers and other travellers, people in the middle of long journeys who just wanted something hot and quick to eat before continuing on their way.

People who didn't know better, in other words.

Jack, Oscar, Ruby and Snivel walked

towards the café. Once, Ruby sniffed, but when she saw the way Snivel was looking at her she stopped.

"What *is* that smell?" demanded Oscar as they got closer to the café.

"Greasy Joe's bins," said Jack. "Probably the location of the most disgusting food in the country!" He pointed to a pair of black wheelie bins behind the restaurant, on the other side of a high wire fence.

Snivel cocked his head. "I thought you said the disgusting food was *inside?*"

"Yeah," replied Jack, "it is. But all the stuff that's too revolting to eat – even by the kind of people desperate enough to order food here – all that waste ends up in the bins."

"Gross," muttered Ruby. "Are you saying we need to search the bins?"

Jack looked down at Snivel who was trotting along on his lead.

"What do you think, Snivel?" he asked.

"I think this collar is too tight and you keep yanking on the lead!"

"I meant about the Flartibug and the bins?

Do you think the alien could be hiding there?" Once again Jack pointed to the bins. They were surrounded by black bin bags that had split open, spilling their rotting contents all over the ground.

The perfect habitat for a Flartibug.

"It does seem the most likely place," said Snivel as Jack bent down and adjusted the dog collar.

"Let's go then."

Jack began to lead them towards the front door of the café.

"Do we have to go in there?" asked Ruby. "I thought we were going round the back, to the bins?"

"We are," said Jack. "But the only way to get to the back is through the café. Look at that fence – even *you* couldn't climb it."

Ruby looked at the fence that surrounded the site. It was topped with vicious-looking barbed wire. "Well…" she said. "I'd give it a go. But probably best to go through the front door like you said."

As they walked towards the café the door opened and a figure emerged wearing a

uniform. He was
clutching a massive
burger from which
bits of greasy
sauce and onion
were dripping. The
man took a large

bite out of the burger and then stopped dead,
seeing the three children coming towards
them.

His eyes widened as he recognised the kids.
At the same moment Jack and his friends
were also remembering where they had seen
this face before.

"It's the park keeper!" said Oscar. During
their searches for both of the aliens that they
had captured so far they had run into the
park keeper at their local park. Almost
literally. Once, they had accidentally bundled
him up in a net, thinking he was an alien.

The park keeper had obviously not forgotten. He took a long look at the three children, and then dropped his burger and ran away with a terrified expression on his face.

Ruby stared at the discarded burger where it lay on the pavement, its greasy slice of meat and odd, brightly coloured sauces exposed where the top part of the bun had slipped off.

"Maybe I'll become a vegetarian," she muttered.

Inside the café there was an overpowering smell of greasy meat. A large sweaty man in a dirty white apron stood behind the counter and behind him was a massive grill, dripping with fat and covered in black bits of burnt food. There were tables with red-and-white checked plastic tablecloths and all the seats were benches with vinyl-covered cushions. Most of

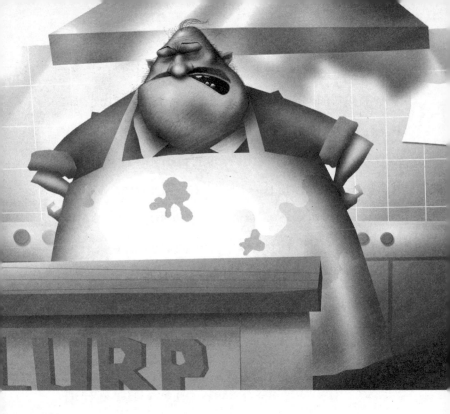

these were ripped and torn, exposing the yellowing foam padding within.

"You'll have to leave the dog outside," said the man as they entered. "It's a hygiene issue."

Looking around the place Jack couldn't help thinking that there were more pressing hygiene issues that the man might care to deal with but, wisely, he said nothing.

"I'll wait outside with Snivel," said Ruby and Oscar almost at the same moment. They then both looked rather embarrassed.

"OK, then you do it," they both said, again at the same time.

Jack handed Snivel's lead to Ruby. "Go on, both of you, I won't be long."

Quickly, before Jack could change his mind, Ruby and Oscar bundled Snivel back outside, leaving Jack to approach the counter.

"What can I do for you?" asked the man.

Jack looked at the menu nervously. "Chips, please," he said finally, "to take away."

The man nodded. "I'll just fry some fresh," he told Jack, pouring some pre-cut frozen chips into some filthy-looking oil in a chip pan. "Be about five minutes."

"Great," said Jack without much conviction. He saw a door leading to the back of the

building where the customer toilets were. "Could I use your loo while I'm waiting?"

The man jerked a thumb in the direction of the door. "Through there."

Jack pushed the door open and found himself in a thin corridor full of half-empty containers of food. There were two doors – marked 'Guys' and 'Dolls' for some reason – and, at the end of the corridor, an external door on which faded red letters spelt out 'Fire Exit'. Jack quickly hurried along the corridor and pushed open the door to the outside.

In the yard behind the café the smell was even worse than it had been from the road. It was overwhelming! Jack coughed and gagged as the odour of rotting vegetables and meat filled his nose. It was the most disgusting thing he had ever smelt. *Surely this was perfect for the Flartibug?*

Something moved at the back of the yard,

behind the bin bags. Bravely Jack crept forwards. He saw a broom lying on the floor and picked it up. Holding it in front of him, like a knight with a lance, he inched closer to where he'd seen the movement. He started using the broom to poke at the pile of bags. At the bottom of the pile was a bunch of rags.

Suddenly the rags moved violently.

"Oy!" they said. Jack stared in amazement. The rags were actually the clothing of a man who had been curled up there asleep. His unshaven and dirty face was contorted in surprise.

This must be the Flartibug in its human disguise! It had taken the form of a tramp, so that it could live here among the bin bags.

Jack took a step back and poked the alien with his broom handle. "Keep back, fiend," he said. "Hand over the Blower part!"

The man stared at him, mouth open. Jack

looked closely at him. The black teeth, the
stubble, the rank breath. It really was a very
good disguise. And he couldn't see a glowing
item anywhere…

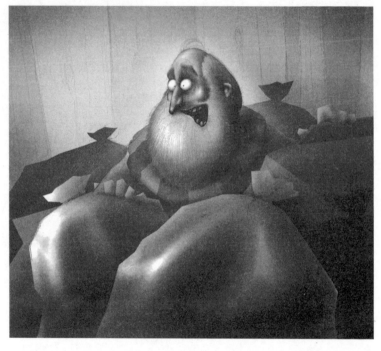

Jack slowly lowered the broom handle.
It really was a tramp!
"Who are you?" asked the tramp. "Leave
my bins alone! This is my patch!"

Before Jack could answer the back door of the café opened and the man who had taken Jack's order appeared.

"What's going on?" he demanded.

"Thanks, pal, this was a nice little place I had 'ere," muttered the tramp, pulling some bags aside in a hurry to reveal a large hole in the fence behind the pile. Moving with more speed than Jack would have believed possible he disappeared through the hole.

"Hey, come back!" shouted the cook. Jack saw that he had a large cooking knife in his hand. Deciding that sometimes running away was the best option, Jack hurried after the tramp through the hole in the fence.

Jack ran at full speed around to the front where Ruby, Oscar and Snivel were waiting.

"Run!" he screamed.

So they ran.

CHAPTER THREE

That night Jack's mum offered to make him his favourite meal for supper – burger and chips. Jack went a funny colour and said that he'd really prefer something else, preferably with vegetables, and maybe some fruit for pudding?

Jack's mum smiled. "Are you on a healthy-eating kick?" she asked. Jack's mum was a nurse at the local hospital and she was always telling Jack not to live on junk food. Unfortunately she was so busy most of the time that they often had to eat ready meals and takeaways. She was really happy to hear Jack demanding something different.

"I just don't fancy a burger tonight," he told her.

"You've been listening to that Ollie James, haven't you?" said his mum with a grin.

Ollie James was a TV chef, famous for two things – being very successful at a very young age and for being outspoken about everything to do with food. Right now he was in the middle of a big campaign to improve the standard of school dinners.

"Oh look, there he is now," said Jack's mum, pointing at the TV which was showing some local news. Jack grabbed the remote control and turned up the volume.

On the screen Ollie James was being interviewed by a familiar face – the ex-*Animal Ark* presenter Zana, whom Jack had met when chasing the Burrapong at the local zoo.

"The fing is," said Ollie in his usual cockney accent, "kids need better nosh at dinner and I'm gonna knock on every school kitchen door until they get it!"

But Jack wasn't listening anymore. He was thinking about aliens who liked disgusting food. Because there were worse things to eat than Greasy Joe's fry-ups, weren't there?

Yes. There were school dinners.

Of course... thought Jack.

How often had he and Oscar been stuck in the school dining hall pushing inedible and unidentified chunks of who-knows-what around their plates hoping they'd be allowed to throw it away and go and play? Most days of the week! If this Flartibug liked disgusting food he'd be bound to head for a school kitchen and, Jack was confident, the most disgusting school kitchen in town was surely the one at—

"Your school!" said his mum suddenly. Jack realised that she had come to stand next to him and was following the interview.

"What?"

"Weren't you listening?" asked his mum. "Ollie's taking his Nosh not Tosh tour on the road to make school dinners better and he's coming to your school – tomorrow! Isn't that exciting?"

"Yeah, brilliant," said Jack quickly. It *would* be brilliant if they started getting better food at school, really brilliant, but not before they'd found and trapped the Flartibug.

The next day at school everyone seemed to have heard the news and there was lots of excitement that Ollie James was coming to their school. Some children were carrying copies of his book *Bish, Bosh, Nosh* hoping to get it signed.

"Do you think he can really make our school dinners better?" asked Ruby as she joined Jack and Oscar in the playground.

"Does he *do* miracles?" joked Oscar.

Jack noticed the small TV van in the staff

car park. "Looks like Zana is here," he said.

"Do you think she'll remember us?" asked Ruby.

Jack shrugged. "We'll soon find out," he said, seeing Zana and her cameraman heading towards them across the playground.

"How do you feel about the Nosh not Tosh campaign coming to your school?" asked Zana without any further introduction, thrusting a microphone under Jack's nose.

"Er… we're all really excited," said Jack. He was surprised that Zana didn't seem to remember him and Oscar and Ruby from the zoo – she had spoken to them for a while before they went off to capture the alien who was impersonating the elephant keeper and feeding on elephant farts.

"That's wonderful," said Zana and turned to the camera, ignoring the kids. "There you have it; there's a real sense of anticipation in the playground this morning, as Ollie James chooses this school to launch the next stage of his Nosh not Tosh campaign."

Jack and his friends hurried past her and into the school building.

"She didn't seem to remember meeting us at the zoo," said Oscar.

"Airhead," said Ruby.

"*Oi!*"

"I mean her," Ruby sighed.

"Oh, all right then."

Jack said nothing but, as the door swung closed behind him he took a quick glance back at Zana. It was hard to be sure as the door slammed shut but he was fairly certain that she was looking directly back at him – and her forehead was creased in a frown.

It wasn't until morning break that Jack, Ruby and Oscar were able to get together again to begin their investigation. Usually children were not allowed in school during break and lunchtime but Ruby had offered to do a job for her teacher and had been allowed to rope in Jack and Oscar to help.

"We've got to go to the kitchens to collect some packaging cardboard which we're going to use in Design and Technology," explained Ruby as they moved through the strangely quiet school corridors.

They reached the kitchens and Ruby told one of the dinner ladies what they were there for. The woman told them to wait and went to collect the packaging.

"Take a good look at all the cooks," said Jack. "We know the aliens use disguise technology but we should be able to spot them now."

The three of them took a few steps into the kitchen area and started looking at the dinner ladies. They looked pretty normal at first glance, although they all seemed rather miserable. Their hands were covered in brightly coloured plasters where they had cut themselves chopping vegetables.

"They have to be bright-coloured plasters so they can be seen in case they fall in the food," explained Ruby.

"Shame – they might improve the flavour!" said Oscar.

In one corner of the room one dinner lady was stirring a big pot of brown-coloured gunge. Her hair looked like it had been carved out of a single piece of plastic, and her eyes seemed to be purple. Her thick, pale arms were too long for her body.

All in all, she looked like a monster that was going to a fancy dress party as a human being.

She put a ladle in and dripped the thick disgusting slop back into the pot. **Plop!** Something large dropped back into the stew.

It looked like it might have been a rat.

Then she glanced around quickly and pulled out another ladle – but this time she raised it to her lips after filling it with the revolting slop. Throwing her head right back at an impossible angle, her throat opened up in a wide, second mouth. Insect-like mandibles appeared from this hole in her neck as she swallowed the foul-looking food.

"That's our alien," muttered Jack, jabbing Ruby in the ribs.

Ruby was looking at
the alien dinner
lady's wrist.

"And that
must be her
Blower part,"
she said, pointing at the
strangely glowing wristwatch that the fake
dinner lady was wearing.

Before they could discuss the matter
further the first dinner lady returned
with an armful of flattened cardboard
boxes. Together the three of them managed
to carry the cardboard back
to Ruby's classroom.

"Meet after school at the jungle trail," said
Jack. "We need to get more intelligence."

"Isn't that what we come to school for?"
asked Oscar.

Ruby bashed him on the shoulder. "He

means data, information, observation. We
need to spy on the alien."

"Oh," said Oscar, rubbing his fresh bruise,
"why didn't you say so?"

When school finished the three friends met, as
planned, at the playground jungle trail and
then sneaked back into school. Taking care to
keep out of sight of any teachers and
cleaners, Jack and his friends made their way
back to the school kitchens where the dinner
ladies were still clearing things away. They
crept into the dining hall itself and
approached the serving hatch. Luckily the
sliding hatch cover was not properly closed.
Jack tried to push it up but it was very heavy.
Oscar and Ruby gave him a
hand and together they
managed to lift the sliding door

up about six centimetres, enough to give them a slit at the bottom through which they could spy on the kitchen.

One by one the dinner ladies said their goodnights to the school cook until only one remained – the one with the glowing wristwatch. The school cook was looking at her own watch.

"Come on, Eileen," she said, "I've got a hair appointment to get to. I want to look my best when that Ollie James interviews me tomorrow..."

"You get off, boss," said the dinner-lady alien, "I'll finish off here."

"Are you sure?" asked the school cook, but

she was already removing her white coat and getting her bags. The alien nodded and the school cook bustled out to get her hair done.

As soon as the door closed behind the cook, the remaining dinner lady started to vibrate and blur. A moment later she stopped and was revealed in her true form. In the flesh the Flartibug was every bit as disgusting as it had looked on Snivel's hologram but somehow

much worse. It was like looking at an insect in a microscope – only the Flartibug wasn't tiny.

It was huge.

The giant insect-like alien lost no time in getting on with what it really wanted – disgusting food. It moved across to the slops bin where all the waste from lunch ended up. Jack regularly tipped most of his lunch into that bin without eating any of it. The alien pulled off the lid and with two of its thin but powerful limbs it lifted the bin clear off the floor and tipped it up. A horrible mixture of half-eaten and congealed food poured out of the bin and into the waiting mouth of the Flartibug, like a dustbin emptying into a council dustcart.

"I think I'm going to be sick," whispered Oscar.

"Don't you dare – she'd probably eat that

too," replied Ruby.

Finally the fetid feast was finished and the alien replaced the bin on the ground. It let out one enormous burp, which filled the room with a quite nauseating stench, and then unfurled a pair of transparent wings like a beetle's and started to fly towards the door. The alien pushed it open and, slightly clumsily, flew off into the sky.

Jack and his friends emerged from their hiding place and watched as the alien disappeared.

"Snivel didn't think it was worth mentioning that it can *fly?*" said Oscar.

"Bit of an oversight," said Ruby. "This is going to make things difficult."

"And where's it gone?" asked Oscar.

"Snivel reckoned it would probably spend the night at a tip somewhere," said Jack. "All

the stuff decomposing keeps it warm, and reminds it of home. But of course, the food here is much worse than anything you'd find at the tip. So it comes here during the day to eat."

"Right. What's the plan then?" asked Ruby.

Jack thought for a moment and then nodded. He put his arms around his friends' shoulders and pulled their heads close to his.

"This time we'll do it in two parts," Jack began to explain. "Listen carefully..."

cHAPTER FOUR

The next day school began with a special
assembly. Mrs Horton, the head teacher,
explained to the whole school that Zana and
her TV crew would be around all day,
interviewing different children about school
dinners and that Ollie James would be in
school as well later in the day.
An excited buzz went round the
hall. A lot of people had been

disappointed when Ollie and Zana had left before lunch the previous day. Mrs Horton told the children that Ollie James would be helping Mrs Salter, the school cook, design new menus for school dinners that would be healthy and good to eat. ("And tasty too, please," whispered Oscar in Jack's ear.)

"We have to make our move today," said Jack later, when they got back to their class. "Once Ollie starts making that kitchen produce decent food..."

"Nosh not Tosh," interjected Oscar, who liked a good slogan, especially if it rhymed.

"Whatever," continued Jack with a sigh, "but once we get that in the kitchen it won't be so attractive to the Flartibug. And if it goes somewhere else to eat we'll have to find it all over again."

"So today's the day then," agreed Oscar. Jack nodded. It was time to put the plan into action. The only trouble was, it was easy to come up with a plan. It was the *action* part that was difficult...

For once Numeracy and Literacy seemed to whizz by and, before he knew it, Jack was lining up in the queue for his school lunch. As he approached the counter he saw that Mrs Salter had clearly made an effort today, knowing the TV cameras were coming in.

It looked like she'd thrown just about every ingredient in the store cupboard into today's dishes, but the result was a bit of a mess. The first dinner lady was ladling out what looked like fresh green vomit. Jack thought it was meant to be some kind of vegetable soup but he couldn't be sure and didn't want to take the risk. He shook his head and moved his tray on. The second dinner lady had an even more disgusting tray of food. This one looked like diarrhoea, a thin brown liquid full of small lumps.

"Curry?" asked the dinner lady hopefully, ladling some up in readiness.

Jack nearly gagged. The dinner lady took that as a no.

Behind him in the dinner hall there was a bit of a commotion going on. Jack looked around and saw that Zana had appeared with her cameraman and Ollie James.

"All right, mate," Ollie said cheerfully to a nervous-looking girl from Year Two. "Whatcha got on your plate today, darlin'?"

The girl just looked at him with her eyes wide open. Jack felt sorry for her – she'd probably never seen someone famous in the flesh before. Undeterred, Ollie moved onto another child, who had a plate of the curry.

"What's that then? Bit of the old Ruby?" he asked the boy.

"I think it's beef, not Ruby," whispered the lad bravely.

"No, no, mate, Ruby Murray. It's rhyming slang for curry. Let's 'ave a taste, eh?" replied Ollie, picking up a spoon and bravely having a mouthful.

The cameraman moved quickly to get a close-up of the

famous chef's face as he tasted the school meal. For once the talkative cook was lost for words. His face screwed up as if he'd stepped on a drawing pin and then he made an expression that looked like his face was melting. Finally he grabbed a beaker of water and downed it in one.

Instantly Zana had the microphone in his face.

"So what do you think?"

Ollie shook his head sadly. "Boy, have we got our work cut out for us here!"

Jack could only agree as he reached the third dinner lady. Her stainless-steel vat contained another kind of stew – but this one was full of what looked like eyeballs!

Are those eggs? thought Jack. *I hope they're eggs.*

Whatever they were, Jack had no intention of letting them near his mouth – but he still offered his tray up for some. Because he had recognised his target.

The dinner lady serving the eyeball stew was the Flartibug – or rather the human form of the Flartibug. She tried to smile at Jack, but the result was ghastly. Her skin didn't really fit her face properly, and it folded in strange ways as her mouth lifted at the sides.

Jack watched with horror as the gloopy mess slopped onto his tray. As the dinner lady reached forward to serve him he kept his eyes on the glowing wristwatch above her hand.

The first part of the plan – getting served by the Flartibug – was underway. Now he just

had to hope he could manage the next step…

"Looks yummy," he said, trying to sound like he meant it.

The alien regarded him with suspicious eyes. *Was the child being sarcastic?*

Jack held her gaze without blinking.

"Can I have some more, please?"

Jack moved his tray back slightly, so that the fake dinner lady had to reach further forward to pour the extra lunch onto his tray.

As soon as her hands were close enough, Jack pounced. Dropping his tray onto the metal rail, he grabbed the alien's wrist with one hand, while with the other he pulled at her watch. Before she could do anything, he had managed to pull the concealed Blower part clear of her arm and slipped it into his pocket.

He glanced around. No one had noticed.

The alien was furious but, as Jack had

hoped, there were too many people around
for her to make a scene. She hissed, and for
just a moment the insect mouth in her neck
opened and her beetle-like jaws clicked
angrily. "Give that back!" she whispered in a
tone of deadly anger.

Jack grinned. "Don't make a fuss; you'll

draw attention to yourself. Do you want to be on TV?"

The alien dinner lady hissed again but said nothing.

"You want this back?"

The alien nodded.

"Then meet me at four in the park down the road," said Jack. Now he had the Blower part – but he still had to trap the alien and deliver her to Bob, if he wanted to complete the mission.

Without another word Jack picked up his tray again – only a little of the stew had spilled when he let go of it – and turned to move away.

But his path was blocked by Zana and her cameraman. How long had they been there? Had she heard any of that?

"Hi there, and what interesting things did you pick up at the food counter today?"

asked Zana brightly, pointing her microphone at him.

Jack hesitated. Something about the way she had phrased that question worried him. Perhaps she had heard or seen something. He decided to try and bluff it out.

"Oh, just the usual," he said, matching her tone.

Ollie James stepped between them.

"Not after today, mate," he said confidently. "We can do better than this and from tomorrow we will. Nosh not Tosh, right, mate?"

"Yeah," said Jack, dumping his tray's contents directly in the slops bin. "Nosh not Tosh!"

Some kids sitting nearby took up the cry and repeated it.

"Nosh not Tosh! Nosh not Tosh!"

Soon the whole dining hall was chanting the slogan. Zana's cameraman panned his camera around, taking it all in. Jack took the opportunity to glance back at the alien dinner lady. He held his hand up with the thumb tucked in. Four. She nodded.

Jack headed for the exit, hungry but happy.

Just as he was about to go through the door, though, he turned and caught Zana's eye. A chill went through him.

Zana did not look like she had not been watching the children chanting, or the cameraman, or Ollie. She was only looking at Jack, then at the alien dinner lady, then back at Jack again. Her mouth was open slightly in shock.

Oh, no, thought Jack. She saw something. And now she's suspicious…

On the other side of the canteen, Zana peered at the boy as he left the room. She had seen and heard everything that had happened between him and the dinner lady – the so-called dinner lady.

And this time, she was determined not to let the story slip out of her grasp.

cHAPTER FIVE

After school Jack almost ran home, to make
final preparations. He picked up his special
helicopter and the remote control. Fixed to the
helicopter was an unusual-looking leather
harness.

"You're sure this will carry your weight?" he
asked Snivel for about the tenth time since the
plan had come together.

"I have checked and rechecked the

calculations," Snivel assured him. "Anyway I'm pretty much indestructible."

"You might be," replied Jack, "but if you fall out of the sky you could do a lot of damage to something or someone else."

They set off for the park.

Jack cast a nervous look up at the sky. There were dark clouds gathering on the horizon and the wind seemed to be picking up.

"Did you check the weather report?" he asked his faithful robot dog.

"There is a storm coming," said Snivel, "but it shouldn't hit until tonight."

"It's going to be tough flying the chopper if this wind gets any stronger."

"It's a good plan," Snivel told him. "What could go wrong?"

Jack didn't answer him. He could think of lots of things that might go wrong.

Jack met Oscar at the park gates. A moment later, Ruby came zooming up to them on her kite-propelled skateboard. There was a stiff wind and, as she approached, the skateboard lifted up into the air before she was able to wrestle the kite down. She skidded to a halt.

"Oops," she said. "Wind's a bit strong to be using an adult-sized kite." Collapsing the kite, she undid her weight belt, then set all the equipment aside.

"Why did you bring that?" asked Jack.

Ruby shrugged. "It won't take long to kick alien butt, will it? We can have a play with this after."

Jack stared at her. "In this wind? I don't fancy going into orbit, thanks."

"You're heavier than me. You'd be fine."

"I'd have a go," said Oscar. "The wind doesn't scare me."

Jack rolled his eyes. "Anyway, I don't know

that it'll be that easy to kick this alien's butt. This one knows we're after it."

Ruby sighed. "You worry too much."

Jack looked around. Most of the people had left the park, heading home to have tea and watch the TV. Jack sort of wished he was doing the same.

But instead he cast a quick look at his watch. Three thirty-five. "Time to get into position."

Jack was looking around. "Any sign of Zana and her cameraman?"

"Why would she be here?"

"I told you – I think she suspects something. She saw what went on at the zoo last time, when we captured the alien in the elephant enclosure, didn't she? And I think she may have seen what happened when I grabbed the Flartibug's Blower part."

Ruby was looking around too now. "It's a big park," she muttered.

"Hey, I've got an idea," said Oscar suddenly.

Jack and Ruby exchanged nervous looks. Oscar's ideas were usually stupid or dangerous and often both.

"Why don't I have a quick go on Ruby's kite thing? I can get around the park really quickly and make sure Zana isn't here."

Jack bit his lip, thinking. "We do need to make sure we're not being watched."

Ruby started giving the safety equipment to Oscar. "Go on then, I know you're dying to have a go anyway."

Oscar started to unfold the kite.

"Wait!" said Ruby. "Put this on first." She handed him the weight belt. "Otherwise you really will fly up into orbit."

A few minutes later, Oscar was ready. Ruby launched the kite and soon Oscar was away, zooming around the park at great speed.

Even with the belt on, he sometimes lifted right up into the air, almost flying, and Jack could hear him whooping with delight.

Jack watched him go. Ruby looked at Jack.

"You really think we're being watched?" she asked.

Jack shrugged. "I've just got a feeling, that's all."

In fact, Jack and his friends *were* being watched. Close by where Jack was standing a small squirrel was

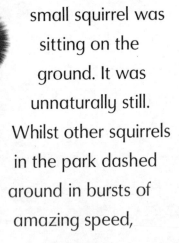

sitting on the ground. It was unnaturally still. Whilst other squirrels in the park dashed around in bursts of amazing speed, keeping out of the way of the humans, this squirrel seemed fascinated by the three children. Its little squirrel head turned with mechanical precision to keep its eyes fixed on the three kids.

The squirrel was an artificial life form; like Snivel it was a robot and it was there to keep an eye on Jack and his team. Bob wanted to make sure that everything was going to plan. A signal from the squirrel's eyes was beamed wirelessly to a control box hidden in the branches of a tree from where they were transmitted to Bob's HQ.

Inside his base, Bob watched with nervous anticipation. He had seen that the children had already collected the third Blower part; now they had to capture the alien itself. Bob could hardly breathe. Everything was coming together nicely…

Bob and the Squirrel were not the only people in the park watching the GUNGE agents with a great deal of interest. Hidden in a pile of refuse sacks, Zana was lying on

the damp ground, shivering. She wasn't sure if she was shivering from the cold or from excitement. This was it. This was the moment that she had been dreaming of for so long.

At the zoo, she'd seen something impossible – a strange, insect-like creature being swallowed by an elephant's bum-hole. And today, at the school, she'd seen something else.

She'd seen a dinner lady's neck open up like a mouth, and insect jaws coming out.

And both times, that boy Jack had been there. He'd even arranged to meet the strange dinner-lady-bug-thing here at the park. She'd heard the whole thing.

Zana wasn't sure what was going on. Was it a government experiment gone wrong? Were huge killer insects taking over the town? Or was it an alien invasion?

It didn't matter. One thing was for sure: when she broke this story – with exclusive video footage – her journalistic career would be made. This was her chance and she was determined not to mess it up.

She checked the remote control in her hand. Everything was in order. She had decided that this was too important to share with her cameraman and had therefore 'borrowed' some equipment from his van when he had gone for lunch. Claiming to have a headache she had called an early wrap to the day's scheduled interviews and had left the school while the children were still in lessons. That had given her the opportunity to get to the park early and to conceal two tiny remote-operated cameras at crucial positions. Now all she had to do was wait.

The park keeper was sitting in his hut, eating a sandwich. He'd missed his lunch, because of those blasted children being at Greasy Joe's.

Even thinking about those kids gave him the shivers.

Ever since they had managed to wrap him in a tennis net earlier in the year they had been bad news as far as he was concerned. He glanced up at the television screen fixed in the corner of the hut. It relayed a sequence of shots from four black-and-white security cameras that had been installed by the council recently. It was meant to make his job easier – and it certainly did. Now when the weather was cold or windy he could just stay in his hut with a nice hot thermos of soup and keep an eye on his park from the warm.

As he watched, the automatic system flicked between the four cameras; there was the boating lake, there was the main gates, there were the swings and there—

The park keeper sat bolt upright and nearly choked on the bite of sandwich he had just taken.

It was them! The three kids! The ones who had cost him his lunch and were now ruining his tea break. Enough was enough. Something had to be done!

Jack watched as Oscar roared around on the skateboard pulled by the kite. Ruby joined him.

"Five minutes till the alien gets here," she said. "Time for me to hide."

"Where are you going to be?" asked Jack.

Ruby pointed to a load of black bin bags

lying at the side of the path. "That pile of bin bags is massive. I'll hide behind there, OK?"

Jack nodded. "Good luck!" he added as she headed for her chosen place of concealment.

Jack looked back at his watch. Four minutes to the hour. He wondered if the alien would be on time.

Suddenly he heard a soft flapping noise and then a rasping voice.

"OK, human. There's no one around now. Hand over my Blower part."

Jack turned around slowly. In front of him stood the alien in her human disguise. She was early!

cHAPTER sIx

Jack pulled out his remote control and started up the model helicopter. Immediately the blades began to whirl and the craft started to rise into the air. As it went up it lifted a special harness – and held in the harness was Snivel. Strapped to one of Snivel's paws was the Blower part – the glowing alien watch!

"Sorry, bug-face, I don't seem to have your watch on me," said Jack bravely, although his voice did wobble a bit.

The alien dinner lady hissed in anger.

"My dog's gone for a little spin and, oh, look!" Jack pointed up in the sky. "He seems to have flown off with it!"

Zana, from her hiding place near the bottom of the pile of black bin bags, watched in fascination. The boy named Jack was having an argument with the dinner lady from school – the one who, Zana could swear, had a second mouth in her neck. But he'd also strapped his pet dog to a remote control helicopter, and now he was flying it up into the air.

It was terrible, cruel treatment of a defenceless animal!

And it would make great TV.

Zana had hidden tiny

cameras around the park. Now she operated the remote control in her hand to get one of them to zoom in on Jack and the dinner lady.

The small handheld monitor showed the image as it became more detailed. The dinner lady seemed to be shaking, vibrating. *Was there something wrong with the camera?* The outline of the woman started to blur and then, suddenly, the picture snapped back into focus and Zana had to stop herself from screaming. The woman was gone and in her place was some kind of giant insect!

The furious Flartibug, now in its true form, launched itself into the sky with its thin insect

wings beating rapidly. There was a lack of
elegance as the creature
wobbled into the air. *Must have
just been stuffing her face,*

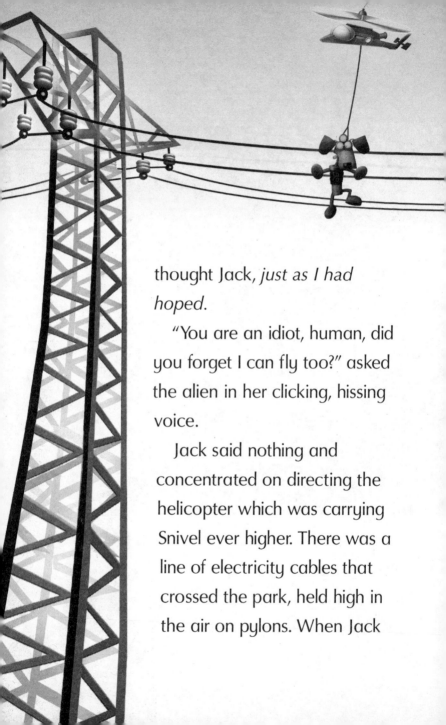

thought Jack, *just as I had hoped*.

"You are an idiot, human, did you forget I can fly too?" asked the alien in her clicking, hissing voice.

Jack said nothing and concentrated on directing the helicopter which was carrying Snivel ever higher. There was a line of electricity cables that crossed the park, held high in the air on pylons. When Jack

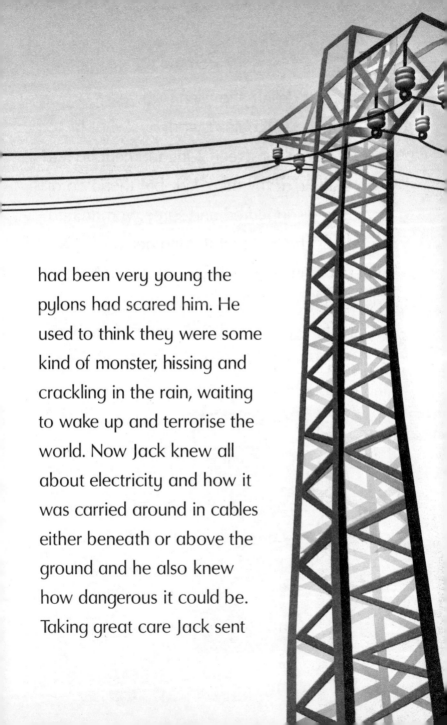

had been very young the pylons had scared him. He used to think they were some kind of monster, hissing and crackling in the rain, waiting to wake up and terrorise the world. Now Jack knew all about electricity and how it was carried around in cables either beneath or above the ground and he also knew how dangerous it could be. Taking great care Jack sent the helicopter on a course towards the nearest pylon. To his delight the alien followed.

The park keeper couldn't work out what he was seeing on his screen. One moment he had been looking at the three kids but then two of them had disappeared and some woman had turned up. The constant flicking between the cameras made it easy to get confused but this was ridiculous.

Now the woman had gone, one of the boys was playing with a remote control and some kind of horribly ugly insect was flying really

close to one of his cameras.

The park keeper grabbed a rake – just in case – and hurried out of his shed.

Jack had to really concentrate now. He wanted Snivel and the helicopter to get close to the pylon but not too close. He had to take his eye off the alien. Suddenly he was aware of a blur of movement. *Was it Ruby? Oscar?*

No, it was the Flartibug. She had changed direction suddenly and was diving towards the ground and towards... Jack! Before he had a chance to protect himself the alien had wrapped two of its spindly legs around him and pulled him into the air.

"Did you think I could be fooled so easily? I know you've caught two of my… colleagues… but I'm smarter than any blithering Burrapong or stupid Squillibloat!" said the alien proudly.

The Flartibug continued to climb into the air. Jack watched in horror as the ground fell away.

"I am a Flartibug and I am no fool," hissed the creature. "Now bring me my part of the Blower or I will drop you

Jack tried to calculate how far up they were now. *Twenty metres? Thirty metres?* Did it really matter? He'd be dead just the same.

This is it, thought Zana. This was the footage that would make her famous. This was going to be big. Bigger than *Newsround*. Bigger

than *News at Ten*. This was going to be
global.

Just need to make sure I get the best shots.
Zana remembered something
one of her producers had told
her when she had first worked

in television. "You can say what you want on television but it only means something to the viewer when they can actually see it. Pictures are the most important bit!"

She wriggled forward so that the remote poked out from under the pile of bin bags, to ensure the signal was clear.

Jack swallowed hard. What was he to do? This far from the ground it was getting very windy, making it even harder to control the helicopter. Snivel was being buffeted around in the gusts of wind.

Frantically Jack worked the remote controls, trying to prevent the chopper flying into the electricity pylon.

The Flartibug looked at the remote control in Jack's hands, then at the helicopter and Snivel suspended beneath it.

"Ah, I see that you are controlling your flying pet with that thing!" it said. Then it leaned in close, grinning at him through its horrible insect mouth. Its breath stank of rotting filth. "Now," it said, "you will use that device to crash your pet into the ground!"

"What?" exclaimed Jack.

"You heard me, human. Sacrifice your pet and I may choose not to drop you to your certain death."

"What do you mean you *may* choose not to drop me?" demanded Jack.

"Well, it might be fun to watch... But make your dog's crash spectacular enough, and I shall probably be satisfied."

Jack fought his rising panic. *What to do?*

"Getting bored now," said the alien.

Jack thought desperately. If he crashed the chopper Snivel could be flattened... but if he

refused to do as the Flartibug demanded it would be him plummeting towards the grounds and getting spread out across most of the park. *What to do?*

"Time's up," clicked the alien.

With another of its thin hairy limbs the Flartibug snatched the remote control from Jack's hands and tossed it into the air.

"Goodbye, doggy!" it said, laughing.

CHAPTER SEVEN

From behind the bin bags Ruby had been watching the whole episode unfold with mounting horror. The plan was not going well. She would have to do something. But what? It was all happening up in the air and she was on the ground. What could she do? Then she saw the remote control for the helicopter falling out of the sky. If that smashed, the chopper would be out of control. Snivel wouldn't have a chance.

Almost without thinking, Ruby jumped up and climbed over the bin bags in three quick leaps.

She didn't notice that the third bin bag she landed on went "oof!"

That was because it wasn't a bin bag at all – it was Zana. Winded, the television presenter

SMASH!

dropped her camera-operating remote.

Ruby jumped from Zana's back to the ground, not noticing the remote control under her feet either.

Zana couldn't believe it. Suddenly something had jumped on her back. Was it another monster? She couldn't see as her face was squashed into the muddy ground. She felt her remote control fall out of her hand and then heard it smash as something heavy landed on it.

She no longer had a way to control the cameras but she still had her monitor. The signal from the cameras was being wirelessly beamed to her monitor's hard drive. As long as she had that she had her evidence.

Jack watched the helicopter

remote falling away.

"**No!**" he screamed.

Suddenly he was aware of a movement in the air near him. It was Oscar! Oscar was flying?

"I undid the belt!" screamed Oscar, seeing the confusion on Jack's face. *Of course,* Jack thought, *Oscar's using Ruby's kite-board.* Jack saw the way Oscar was sailing clumsily through the air, the kite acting like a flying machine.

Oh, no, he thought. *He's taken off the weight belt, the idiot…*

Without the belt holding it down, the adult kite had snatched Oscar into the air and now here he was flying to Jack's rescue. Oscar grabbed hold of Jack and

wrestled him free of the alien's grasp. The added weight instantly made the kite fly

lower. The pair of them began to spin towards the ground.

Ruby was running but her eyes were looking up. The chopper remote was falling fast now. She had to time this just right. Luckily Ruby played a lot of hand-eye coordination sports. If anyone could catch the remote safely it was her.

A sudden gust of wind caught the remote, causing her to miscalculate. She wasn't going to get underneath it in time. There was only one option. Ruby launched herself into the air, stretching out her hands in front of her like a goalkeeper trying to save a penalty. Time seemed to stand still. In super-slow motion Ruby seemed to float through the air, her fingers reaching forward and then – SLAP! – the remote landed in her outstretched hands and – **THUMP!** – she hit the floor.

Ruby rolled over to take in the situation above her. Oscar was up in the air, the kite flapping in the wind.

Oh, no, she thought. The idiot's taken off the weight belt…

Then Oscar slammed into Jack, grabbing him from the Flartibug, and then the two of them were spiralling towards the ground.

Meanwhile, Snivel was still hanging from the harness under the chopper, dangerously close to the electricity cables, and the Flartibug was flying towards him!

Quickly, Ruby worked at the controls, bringing the chopper lower. She needed to get Snivel beneath the alien to trap it but she couldn't be sure that the voice activation would work at this distance.

Oscar and Jack could see what she was doing. As soon as Ruby got the chopper underneath the alien they all shouted out in unison: **"AGTIVATE SNIVEL TRAP!"**

The alien technology inside Snivel performed the transformation and the dog

turned into a sleek steel box which sucked the alien in like a vacuum cleaner. SLAM! The trap's door clanged shut. They'd done it!

"Oy! What do you think you're doing?"

It was the park keeper running towards them. He didn't seem at all happy at the things that were happening in his park. He waved his rake at them angrily.

"Keep off the grass!" shouted the park keeper pointing towards a sign that Ruby had completely ignored. Ruby realised that she had intruded onto the park's bowling green.

She was about to apologise but before she could say anything Oscar and Jack came into view just behind the park keeper. The wind was getting quite wild now and it was hard for Oscar to control the kite.

Luckily they managed to find a soft landing place.

Unluckily for the park keeper,

he was the soft landing place!

He just had time to look up at the kids falling towards him from the sky. *How did they get up there?* He thought. *Blasted kids…*

And then they were on top of him. His rake was knocked out of his hand and landed some distance away on the path.

Oscar and Jack untangled themselves from the kite. The park keeper was out cold but otherwise unhurt.

Her face covered with mud, Zana crawled out from under the pile of bin bags and got to her feet. She was cold, wet and dirty but she was triumphant. In her hand she held the TV monitor which would make her career. The pictures stored on the device's hard-drive would prove her story. No one would be able to doubt her word.

She staggered forward, stiff from the long time she had been lying on the damp ground. With mud all over her face she couldn't really see properly. She had no idea that the park keeper's rake had landed on the path in front of her. No idea, that is, until she stepped on the metal end, causing the long wooden handle to snap into the air and hit her squarely on the forehead. Zana fell to the floor, instantly unconscious, and completely oblivious to the fate of her precious TV monitor which flew through the air and landed on the ground.

Nearby the robotic eyes of the squirrel were watching carefully. In his base Bob watched the Squirrel-Cam with great interest and some considerable apprehension. If the journalist got those pictures on the television the whole GUNGE operation might be uncovered. It couldn't happen.

Bob stood by, waiting to issue instructions to the squirrel to get the monitor. Then he began to grin. It looked like it might not be necessary. The children were bringing Snivel – in his trap mode – back to earth. The chopper came to rest on the ground. Directly over the monitor that Zana had dropped. **SMASH!** Bob could see that the device was totally destroyed. Without meaning to,

Jack and his friends had even solved that problem for him!

Hurrah for the agents of GUNGE!

CHAPTER EIGHT

The next day was a day Jack and his school friends would remember for a long time. Ollie James took control of the school kitchens and lunch was absolutely...

"Delicious!" said Jack, wiping his mouth on the sleeve of his school jumper.

"Brilliant," agreed Ruby, finishing off the last bit of chicken fricassée.

Oscar was still chewing. "Nosh not Tosh!"

he said with his mouth full of food, which made a revolting sight but was nevertheless truthful.

It looked like school dinners would never be the same again. Ollie James was personally going to rewrite all the school cook's menus and train the dinner ladies to make the new recipes.

"I guess any more Flartibugs that come this way will need to find somewhere else to get their disgusting food," said Ruby grinning.

"I just thought of something," said Jack. "I wonder what Bob does with the aliens that we keep catching?"

"Maybe we should ask him?" suggested Oscar.

Jack nodded. "Maybe we should."

Somewhere else, in a place

where the usual rules of space and time seemed to have been suspended, the subject of the children's discussion was in his base, checking on their progress so far.

Well, he was about to check on progress. Right now he was pushing three ten-pound notes through the little slot. That was the problem with living in a cash point. People

kept expecting cash.

Still, it was better than when he'd been in the postbox and heavy packages had kept falling on him.

And the less said about his time in a bin, the better.

Finally, the money was taken, and Bob saw that there was no queue for the machine. He turned and went deeper into his lair. Inside the base was a long dark corridor of glass-walled cells, three of which were now occupied. At the end of the corridor was a sort of trophy cabinet with four spaces. Three of the platforms were lit and contained the parts of the Blower the children had obtained from the Squillibloat, the Burrapong and the Flartibug. One platform remained unlit and empty.

The kids had delivered the Flartibug late last night. As usual they had brought the

Snivel Trap to his latest location and Bob had taken the captured alien and put it in one of his cells. He had then returned Snivel to his dog form and sent him back to Jack. He would need Snivel one more time.

Just one more, thought Bob to himself, *one more alien, one last Blower part...*

Bob wandered back to his control room to check reports from his various agents and spies. The robot squirrel was not the only

operative he had in the field. Nor were Jack and his friends the only agents.

Bob found that everything was in place. Everything was running according to plan and according to schedule. It was time for the final move of the game.

Earth's future would be decided, one way or the other...

And it would be very soon now.

THE FOURTH GROSSLY FUNNY GUNK ALIENS ADVENTURE!

Jack and his friends are nearing the end of their mission, with only one alien left to capture. The best is always saved for last, though, so none of them should be surprised that this particular alien loves only one thing… poo! But at least, once they've made a sickening descent into the sewers, the world should finally be safe. Shouldn't it?

JOIN THE FIGHT IF YOU VALUE YOUR SNOT!

JONNY MOON
GUNK ALIENS

Buy more great Gunk Aliens books direct from HarperCollins
at 10% off recommended retail price.
FREE postage and packing in the UK.

The Verruca Bazooka	ISBN 978 0 00 731094 4
The Elephant's Trump	ISBN 978 0 00 731095 1
The Dog's Dinner	ISBN 978 0 00 731096 8
The Sewer Crisis	ISBN 978 0 00 731097 5

All priced at £4.99

COMING SOON

Gunk Aliens 5 & 6

To purchase by Visa/Mastercard/Switch simply call
08707871724 or fax on **08707871725**